powerful man in the universe and the protector of Castle Grayskull. Prince Adam's pet tiger Cringer turned into the mighty Battle Cat, He-Man's faithful companion.

Only Orko, the court magician, and Man-at-Arms, He-Man's best friend, knew this secret. Even Prince Adam's parents and Teela, captain of the guard, saw him only as the prince of Eternia. Prince Adam kept his secret because danger lived on Eternia.

On one side of the planet, the sun never shined. There, inside Snake Mountain, the wicked Skeletor planned new ways to find

out Castle Grayskull's secrets. And still others with bad intentions waited on other worlds, ready to disturb Eternia's peaceful way of life.

Against them all stood only He-Man and the Masters of the Universe!

THE HORDE

Written by Bryce Knorr

Illustrated by Harry J. Quinn and James Holloway

Creative Direction by Jacquelyn A. Lloyd

Design Direction by Ralph E. Eckerstrom

A GOLDEN BOOK

Western Publishing Company, Inc.
Racine, Wisconsin 53404

Library of Congress Catalog Card Number 84-62348
ISBN 0-932631-05-3
A B C D E F G H I J

Classic™ Binding U.S. Patent #4,408,780
Patented in Canada 1984.
Patents in other countries issued or pending.
R. R. Donnelley and Sons Company

"**I** have dreamed of this since I first came to Eternia," Skeletor said at his home in Snake Mountain.

"**I've worked for years. At last, I can use what I stole from Hordak so long ago!**

"**Nothing can stop me now! Nothing!**"

Skeletor waved his hand. The box in front of him opened. A bright, purple light shone onto Skeletor.

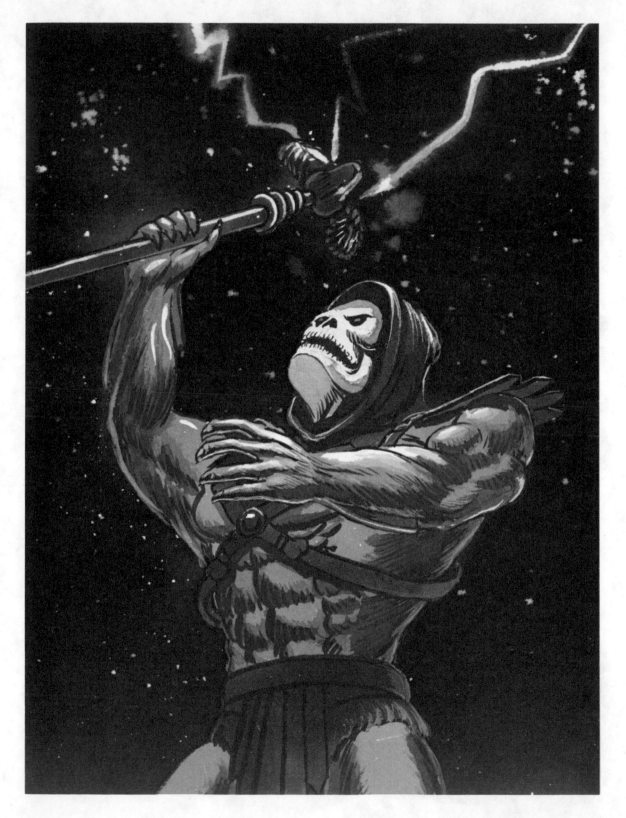

Skeletor threw back his head and laughed.

"I have never felt this strong!" he shouted.

"The Etheramite in this box will help me to learn all of the secrets of Castle Grayskull."

"Then I will go to Etheria. I will not stop until that world is mine, too. I will be king of the entire universe!"

Skeletor banged his Havoc Staff. His men and machines appeared beside him.

He climbed into Spydor and banged his staff again. The army was taken to Castle Grayskull.

"Now to begin my final fight against Castle Grayskull," Skeletor said.

6

Meanwhile, Prince Adam worked very hard at his lessons with Man-at-Arms.

"What is the worst thing in the Vine Jungle, Prince Adam?" Man-at-Arms asked.

"Man-eating plants," Prince Adam answered.

"That is right," Man-at-Arms said. Prince Adam heard another voice he knew.

"He-Man must come to Castle Grayskull quickly," Sorceress told Prince Adam. "Skeletor fights with great power. Please hurry!"

Prince Adam closed his school book.

"Sorceress needs He-Man, Man-at-Arms," he said.
"I must go quickly."

Prince Adam pointed his Power Sword at Cringer.

"D-d-don't I have to stay after school?" his pet tiger asked.

Prince Adam raised the Power Sword high above his head.

"By the power of Grayskull," Prince Adam began.

"I HAVE THE POWER!"

He-Man rode Battle Cat faster than ever before. They found Skeletor's men all around Castle Grayskull. Blast after blast shook Sorceress' home.

"I've never seen Skeletor so strong," He-Man said. **"Somehow, we must stop him."**

"No time to use the front door," Battle Cat growled. "We will go over the top."

Battle Cat jumped over Skeletor like a rocket. With He-Man aboard, he was almost over the wall when Spydor fired. The loud boom shook the very air. The blast sent He-Man and Battle Cat flying over the wall. They landed in front of the Sorceress.

"**That wasn't pretty,**" He-Man said.
"**But we made it. Good job, Battle Cat.**"

"I hope you are in time, He-Man," Sorceress said. "Fighting Skeletor is taking my power."

"We'll do our best," He-Man said.

"We'll teach Skeletor a lesson," Battle Cat growled.

Far away, on another world, a cold voice laughed.

"So Skeletor found out how to use the Etheramite he took from me. Ha! That Etheramite has let my sensors find you, Skeletor. It is time the teacher punished his student."

The voice shouted a command to its warriors.

"Open the portal to Eternia! Show Skeletor the great power of The Horde!"

He-Man used all his might against Skeletor. But nothing worked.
"Take this, He-Man," Skeletor said.
"Taste the power of Etheramite."

A mighty roar shook the air. But it did not come from Skeletor. Instead, Skeletor and He-Man saw a spaceship. It was made from a beam of light!

"At last I found you, Skeletor!" said a voice from the light ship. "Do you remember your teacher? Do you remember the one to whom you lied?"

"No! It can't be!" Skeletor cried. He and all his men disappeared.

"You will not get away," the voice said. The ship faded. "I will punish you!"

The jawbridge to Castle Grayskull opened. Sorceress stepped out to meet He-Man.

"What happened?" He-Man asked.

"Eternia is in great danger, He-Man," she said. "Not only is Skeletor our enemy. Another comes to fight Castle Grayskull.

"He is called Hordak. He already rules one world. He must not rule Eternia, too!"

Back at the palace, Man-at-Arms could not believe Prince Adam's words.

"A Light Cruiser!" he said. "This Hordak must be very strong and powerful, indeed."

Teela ran into the room.

"Father, come quickly! We are under attack from a spaceship. A spaceship made of...*light*!"

"Hordak has come to visit us sooner than we thought," Man-at-Arms said. "Let's go!"

Prince Adam waited until Teela and Man-at-Arms had left. He pulled out his Power Sword.

"I'll need all of Castle Grayskull's power to fight Hordak," he said grimly. **"And perhaps more."**

"By the power of Grayskull," he cried.

"I HAVE THE POWER!"

Hordak's Light Cruiser cast a grim shadow over the palace. He-Man faced four ugly beasts.

"I am Modulok. The more I fight, the stronger I grow. I add new parts to my body until I win!"

"I am Grizzlor. I guard The Horde's jail. No one gets away from me!"

"I am Leech. I can run up and down
and all around. When I touch you,
I draw away your power!"

"I am Mantenna. My wicked eyes
see all. With me looking out for enemies,
The Horde never loses!"

"You won't like my jail, He-Man," Grizzlor said. He snapped at He-Man with his teeth.

"Do not hurt him!" Mantenna said. "We have our orders."

They trapped He-Man on all sides. A beam of light flashed from Hordak's ship. The Horde and their prisoner disappeared!

He-Man stood before an awful creature.

"Welcome, He-Man," Hordak said. "To the Fright Zone. The Light Cruiser is my portal to other worlds."

All around him was a dome of pure Etheramite. Beyond it lay another world—Etheria.

"Bow before Hordak," Grizzlor said.

"I bow only to good, not to bad," He-Man said.
"Why did you bring me here, Hordak?"

"It took me years to find Skeletor," Hordak said. "I tracked him to Eternia. But he is using some trick. I can't find his castle.

"Where can I find him? Tell me!"

"I only answer questions if you say 'please,'" He-Man said. **"And that sounds like a word you don't know."**

"I will teach you Hordak's rules," Hordak said. "Actually, I have only one. Obey!"

Hordak fired toward He-Man. He-Man blocked the blast with his Power Sword. He jumped over Hordak's men and tried to escape. But the Etheramite dome stopped him.

"My Power Sword will cut through that," he said.

"Don't do it!" Hordak said. "I could destroy your power He-Man. But I need you.

"Let me tell you why I brought you here."

Hordak pointed. A picture formed in the air.

"Etheria was once like your home, Eternia," Hordak said.

"The people were happy. But they were not strong. It was easy for us to take over.

"We learned a great secret. Etheria is full of Etheramite, the mightiest mineral in the universe. But the Etherians did not know how to use it.

"Only one young Etherian, Skeletor, wanted this power. I became his teacher. He learned all about wickedness. He learned how The Horde frightens all who see it.

"Together, Skeletor and I learned all about Etheramite. I became stronger than ever. But Skeletor was too young to master its secrets.

"One night, he tried anyway. The Etheramite turned him into a living skeleton. He took some of my Etheramite and looked for his own world to rule.

"Now, Skeletor has finally learned how to use the power of Etheramite. We must stop him. Follow The Horde, He-Man. I will make you stronger than you ever dreamed! If you do not, Skeletor will defeat you!"

"Hordak may be right about Skeletor's power," He-Man thought to himself.
"But there must be a better way. Must I work with evil to fight the wicked Skeletor?"

"I'll think about it," He-Man told Hordak.
"But I need time."

"One hour," Hordak said. "Then you will work with me. Or else!"

He-Man returned to his father's palace on Eternia.

"We don't have much time," He-Man said. He told his friends what had happened.

"...So you see," He-Man ended his story. **"Etheramite gives Hordak the power to go from his world to our world. And now Skeletor knows all about how to use the Etheramite."**

Suddenly, Skeletor appeared before him.

"What are you doing here?" He-Man asked.

"He-man," Skeletor said.

"You must help me stop Hordak. Do you think I am strong now? I have only a little Etheramite. Hordak has a whole planet full of it.

"Join me, He-Man. You have no other choice."

Skeletor's shadowy body disappeared.

"I wonder," He-Man said.

"Both Hordak and Skeletor say we don't have a chance. Maybe there is a way out.

"I must go to Castle Grayskull. If anyone can help us, Sorceress can."

Wind Raider screamed through the sky. Soon Castle Grayskull was in sight.

"You did well, He-Man," Sorceress said. "You found part of the puzzle. We know what has made Skeletor so strong. Now, you must find a way to overcome both of them.

"There is an entrance to the Fright Zone deep in the Vine Jungle. Go there, and whatever happens, don't be afraid."

He-Man walked bravely through the Vine Jungle. A large plant opened its mouth. Without warning, it ate He-Man!

"I will not be afraid," He-Man said. He did as Sorceress told him. He was taken to Grizzlor's jail in the Fright Zone.

"Sorry I can't stay, Grizzlor," He-Man said. He broke the bars with one mighty swing.

He-Man ran to the edge of the Etheramite dome that protected the Fright Zone. He raised his Power Sword high.

"You didn't want me to do this, Hordak," He-Man said. **"So let's see what happens."**

The Fright Zone shook. The Etheramite's power sent He-Man and The Horde crashing through space on Hordak's Light Cruiser. They landed at Snake Mountain!

"Thank you, He-Man," Hordak said. "You changed my plans. But I found Skeletor!

"My Light Cruiser went toward Skeletor when you broke the Etheramite dome. It sought Skeletor's Etheramite.

"Now, I'll show you what I do to those who trick me. We will start with you, He-Man. Then it will be my old pupil's turn."

But touching the Etheramite dome had made He-Man even stronger. Hordak and the rest of The Horde could not beat the powerful He-Man.

"I'm not sure what happened," He-Man said.

"But your Etheramite has helped me, too, Hordak. I just hope it hasn't made me as mean as you are."

Skeletor saw the fight from the top of Snake Mountain. He laughed at his enemies.

"They will take care of each other," he told Two-Bad. **"I won't have to lift a finger. But I want a better view."**

Skeletor held his Havoc Staff toward his enemies. He-Man and The Horde were taken inside Skeletor's arena.

"That's better," Skeletor laughed. ***"Now, on with your fight."***
Hordak was angry.

"I cannot win, He-Man, without using up my power," Hordak said. "Even now, we are too weak to go back to Etheria.

"But with your power, Skeletor, we can make it home. Show him, Leech."

Leech leaped at Skeletor and sapped his power. Skeletor's Etheramite was gone.

"We can leave you now," Hordak said. "I know you won't harm me, He-Man. You are too *good.* But we will come back."

Hordak reopened the portal to Etheria. The Horde disappeared.

"My Etheramite is gone!" Skeletor cried.
"My chance to rule Etheria, gone, because of you, He-Man."

Skeletor ran at He-Man. He-Man just held his Power Sword out to block Skeletor.

"You won't fight me now, Skeletor," he said.
"The Etheramite has made me stronger than ever."

    Back at the palace, He-Man learned that the power from Etheramite did not last.

    "That's why Hordak had to return when he did," Prince Adam explained to Man-at-Arms.

"If he didn't, he'd be stuck here on Eternia forever."

    "What a scary thought," Man-at-Arms said.

"**Skeletor is bad enough,**" Prince Adam said. "**But I would not want Hordak for a teacher.**"

"Teachers and students must trust each other," Man-at-Arms said.

"**That's right,**" Prince Adam agreed. "**Good teachers want to help their students. The two can be friends for life.**"

THE END